The Junior Novelization

Special thanks to Sarah Buzby, Cindy Ledermann, Ann McNeill, Dana Koplik, Emily Kelly, Sharon Woloszyk, Tanya Mann, Julia Phelps, Rita Lichtwardt, Kathy Berry, Rob Hudnut, David Wiebe, Shelley Dvi-Vardhana, Michelle Cogan, Gabrielle Miles, Rainmaker Entertainment, and Walter P. Martishius

www.barbie.com
Published in the United States by Random House Children's Books, a division of Random House, Inc., 1745 Broadway, New York, NY 10019, and in Canada by Random House of Canada Limited, Toronto. Random House and the colophon are registered trademarks of Random House, Inc.
ISBN: 978-0-307-97626-0
randomhouse.com/kids
Printed in the United States of America
10 9 8 7 6 5 4 3 2 1 First Edition

The Junior Novelization

Adapted by Irene Trimble
Based on the original screenplay by
Steve Granat and Cydne Clark

Random House New York

Chapter 1

On a warm summer night in the kingdom of Meribella, an enormous crowd filled the royal amphitheater. The stage was dark, and the crowd was cheering wildly in anticipation. Then, out of the darkness, a voice shouted, "Hello, Meribella! Let's give a warm welcome to the princess of pop . . . the one, the only, the fabulous—Keira!"

The crowd roared, and suddenly, the amphitheater's neon lights flashed on. Giant screens displayed three close-up videos of Keira, all moving in slow motion to a thumping beat. The lights flashed faster as the music grew louder and louder.

Spotlights from every direction converged at one point on the stage. The crowd howled with excitement as Keira rose through the floor on a hydraulic lift. She was dressed in a flashy purple skirt with matching knee-high boots. Even her hair and her microphone were purple! Feeling powerful and in control, the seventeen-year-old pop star gazed out at the screaming crowd. Four female dancers joined her onstage. Then, as fireworks exploded, Keira burst into her hit song "Here I Am."

"Here I am,
Being who I want,
Giving what I got.
Never a doubt now.

"Here I go,
Burning like a spark,
Light up the dark
Again."

Fans danced in the aisles as Keira put on a spectacular show.

At the same time, in a beautiful castle overlooking the amphitheater, a royal reception was taking place. But the music at this event was much quieter.

Violins were playing softly as formally dressed dignitaries entered the castle's Great Hall. An ice sculpture of a gardenia, the kingdom's official flower, graced the center of the glittering room.

The royal family stood at the foot of a marble staircase in an elegant reception line. Seventeen-year-old Princess Tori was at the end of the line. She was lovely in her ball gown, with a tiara in her long blond hair. She looked like a perfect princess. She extended her hand graciously to her guests as they slowly moved down the line.

Tori tried not to seem fidgety and distracted, but there was someplace else she really wanted to be. She looked around mischievously, then grabbed the hand of a nearby guest. She guided the confused woman to take her place in the line.

"Just smile and nod," Tori whispered.

The guests bowed to Tori's replacement with barely a double take while Tori slipped off to the balcony. As she stepped out into the night air, she could hear the music from Keira's concert coming from the amphitheater. Tori leaned over the railing eagerly and began to sing along.

Onstage, Keira sang and danced amid the sweeping lasers, pyrotechnics, and strobe lights. Then she stepped backstage and whispered into her handheld microphone. In a flurry of sparkles, the microphone magically changed Keira's outfit and she emerged wearing a dazzling new pink and blue costume!

Tori gazed toward the amphitheater as she quietly sang. Suddenly inspired, she leaped up onto a chair. Using a candelabra as an air guitar, she sang "Here I Am" as loudly as she could.

"Here I am,
Being who I want,
Giving what I got.

Never a doubt now.

"Here I go,
Burning like a spark,
Light up the dark
Again.
Again, again, again, again and again and
again . . ."

"Princess Tori!" said a stern voice. "What do you think you are doing out here?"

Tori spun around, almost losing her balance. She met the steely glare of her aunt, Duchess Amelia, who was standing in the doorway with her arms folded across her chest. Tori gasped and stepped off the chair.

"Aunt Amelia!" said Tori as she placed the candelabra back on the table. "Oh, please, can't I go down to the concert, just for a little bit?"

"Absolutely not. We have guests. Now come. And please do something with your hair! It's completely inappropriate!" The duchess wheeled around and marched inside.

Tori sighed and dug a hairbrush out of her pocket. "Royal Reception Number Nine," she said to the brush. In an instant, the hairbrush sent a cloud of sparkles glittering around her head as it transformed her long hair into a formal updo. One last time, she looked wistfully toward the concert below; then she headed back inside.

Chapter 2

Chamber music was still playing as guests mingled in the Great Hall of the palace. Tori rejoined the royal family in the reception line. Her father, King Frederic, a kindly, gray-haired man, greeted the dignitaries warmly. Tori's little sisters, Princess Meredith and Princess Trevi, curtsied politely. Duchess Amelia stood across from them all, carefully monitoring the princesses with a critical eye.

An aristocratic woman named Lady Hamilton moved forward in the line and faced the king. "Your Majesty," she said as she curtsied to him.

"So good of you to come, Monika," King Frederic said, smiling.

Tori also smiled graciously and extended her hand. The two younger princesses curtsied, then said in unison, “Pleased to meet you, Lady Hamilton.”

“My, how they’ve grown!” Lady Hamilton gushed, and chatted amiably with the king. Tori looked over at Trevi and saw her standing straight and still.

Feeling mischievous, Tori reached behind Trevi and tickled her. The little girl suppressed a giggle, then secretly tickled Tori back. Tori grinned and hip-bumped Trevi, who hip-bumped Tori—right into a servant passing by with a tray full of shrimp hors d’oeuvres. The three sisters watched in horror as a piece of shrimp sailed off the tray and dropped down the front of Lady Hamilton’s dress!

Lady Hamilton shrieked. Duchess Amelia glared at the girls, and Tori smiled innocently.

As Tori greeted more guests, her thoughts strayed to the concert, and she tried to imagine what she was missing.

As the evening wore on at the castle, the reception line finally broke up. The gardenia ice sculpture in the Great Hall had nearly melted, and guests milled around, making conversation and eating hors d'oeuvres. Tori kept stealing glances out the window to the amphitheater, where Keira's concert was still going on.

After a while, Duchess Amelia clapped three times. "Attention! Attention, everyone! His Majesty would like to say a few words."

The guests quieted down as King Frederic smiled and cleared his throat.

"Thank you, Duchess Amelia. Allow me to thank our honored guests, in particular those who have traveled here from around the globe to attend this historic occasion: Meribella's five hundredth anniversary."

The guests applauded politely, and King Frederic continued. "To celebrate this special occasion, we have arranged a number of events throughout the week, culminating in Saturday's gala Festival of the Gardenias! Perhaps my sister can elaborate."

"With pleasure, Your Majesty," Duchess Amelia said, nodding to the king. She turned to the guests. "Our program this week includes a splendid flower show, a medieval pageant, a palace guard parade, a tall ship procession—"

"And don't forget Keira's concerts!" Tori interrupted. The crowd clapped, and scattered cheers erupted from the finely dressed guests. The duchess looked at them disapprovingly and gave Tori a withering glance.

"Oh, yes," the duchess said with some disdain, "and a series of concerts by this 'Keira' person." Then her face brightened. "And now I have a delightful little surprise for everyone." She stepped over to an artist's easel that was covered with a cloth.

The three princesses exchanged knowing looks, then warily backed toward a drape hanging on a rear wall.

Duchess Amelia was glowing. "I'm pleased to humbly unveil the portrait that the renowned artist Monsieur Pierre has done of me for this historic occasion. I think you'll agree that he has captured the real me." With a grand flourish, she whipped the cover off the easel—and revealed a painting of a donkey in a party hat!

The guests burst into laughter. Even the king was trying not to laugh. But Duchess Amelia was furious. "Tori!" she howled, her face turning a deep purple.

Tori and her sisters disappeared behind the drape, where a hidden wall panel slid open to reveal a secret passageway. All three princesses scurried through the twists and turns of the secret passage, laughing hysterically.

"You had both better scoot to your rooms," Tori told her sisters. "Auntie A will be on the warpath!" The two little girls headed off in one direction, and Tori went in another.

When she reached the end of the passageway, Tori entered her room through a secret wall panel with a poster of Keira on it. She couldn't count how many times that secret door had gotten her out of trouble.

In Tori's elegantly decorated room, posters of Keira covered nearly every wall. A replica of

Keira's electric guitar leaned against her bed. Next to it hung a fluffy feather boa, just like the ones Keira wore onstage. Tori picked up the guitar and wished she could somehow be part of all the excitement at the concert.

Chapter 3

At the amphitheater, Keira dramatically hit the final chord on her glittering guitar. Thunderous cheers and applause rose from the audience as the pop star took multiple bows and bounded offstage, smiling and waving at her fans. Once she was backstage, Keira turned to her stage manager, Nora.

"Walk with me," Keira said in a commanding voice. "Tell Phil to kill the snow on the 'Fiery Ice' intro." Nora nodded and wrote Keira's every word on the clipboard she was carrying. "And hey, the drums came in late again on 'Rock and Rule.' Oh, and remind Kevin that nap time is *after* the show, okay? And what's going on with the sets for the live broadcast?"

Keira marched toward her dressing room,

followed by Nora, who showed her two drawings on the clipboard. "Here are the designs," Nora said. "You want the trees royal purple or Tokyo violet?"

Keira looked at the two colors. "Royal purple," she answered emphatically. "And move my *Pop Mag* interview to Saturday, right after the broadcast. Are those head shots ready for me? And can they smell like lavender this time instead of wig? Ew."

Nora handed Keira a stack of glossy photos, then continued taking notes. "Sign them," she said. "And the wigs come in tomorrow."

Keira's smartphone rang and she answered it. "Talk to me!" she said as she kept walking. "No way! I need the best cameras. Look, this is going to be my first live telecast, so I'd like it to be in focus, okay? Thank you."

Just as Keira hung up, her business manager, Crider, rushed over. "Wonderful show tonight, Keira, dear!" Crider said in his overly flattering way. "Absolutely your best ever! I mean—I had chills!" He continued to gush.

Keira took off her wig, revealing her long brown hair. "Crider, I thought you took care of the cameras!"

"Um, the record company was just a tad concerned about the budget," he answered cautiously. Keira spun around and got in his face.

"Budget?" she said. "Crider, I've been working my tail off for two years without a break to get to this broadcast! It'll take my career to the next level—which makes it massively important that it be perfect! Got it?"

"Perfect! Absolutely! You're so right!" Crider answered through gritted teeth.

"Keira," Nora said, "there's a tea tomorrow at the castle for everyone involved in the Festival. The princess has requested your presence. I smell a photo op!"

Keira stopped for a moment. "The princess? At the castle? Let's do it." Nora scurried off to attend to the details as Keira reached her dressing room door. Just then Keira spotted Daniel, her choreographer.

"Daniel! I need some new choreography for

Saturday's special. Make it something like this," Keira said as she did a fancy new dance step.

Daniel mimicked her steps perfectly and smiled. "You got it, Keira!" He jotted some notes and said, "It'll be your favorite dance routine yet!"

Keira noticed Crider still hanging around. "Crider, is there something else?" she asked, raising an eyebrow.

"Well," Crider began gingerly, "actually, yes. The record company called again tonight. And while they loved, loved, loved the new album photos, they're, um, still wondering when they can hear some of the . . . um . . . songs."

Crider knew he had touched on a sore subject, but Keira suddenly seemed more upset than angry. "As my manager, you told them the songs aren't ready to be heard yet. And that I'll let them know when they are, right?" said Keira.

"That's exactly what I told them," Crider said, nodding. "You know, you work so hard. Perhaps you should take a break, let me run things. Now, back when my name was up in lights—"

But before Crider could go on, Keira said, "Gotta go, Seymour." Then she went inside her dressing room and closed the door.

Crider was left staring at the door. His jaw began to clench. "Please don't call me Seymour," he said angrily.

Inside her dressing room, Keira leaned against the door with a huge sigh, grateful to be alone. Her in-charge manner quickly dissolved. She put her wig on the dressing table and looked around. Her dressing room was filled with cards and flowers. Her dressing table was laden with makeup. There was a row of colorful wigs on one side and a rack of glamorous costumes on the other. It was a room many girls would have envied. But it just made Keira feel overwhelmed. "Guess I better actually write those songs, huh, Riff?" she said wearily.

A playful bulldog puppy stuck his head out of a pile of costumes in the corner. He was happily chewing one of Keira's boots. At the sight of Keira, he dropped the boot and leaped into her arms.

Keira smiled as Riff licked her face. "Okay, time to give it one more try," she said. She set him down and picked up her spare guitar. She stared at it blankly, picking at a few notes and jiggling one foot absentmindedly. Just thinking about writing suddenly seemed intimidating.

Riff barked again, hoping to get Keira to play with the chew toy he'd just picked up. Keira was grateful for the distraction. "Oh, all right, Riff. Get the clog!"

Chapter 4

Inside Meribella Castle, Duchess Amelia was pounding on Tori's door. It was going to be some time before the duchess got over the embarrassment of the donkey painting. "Tori!" she shouted as she continued pounding. "Tori, open the door this instant!"

Tori was sitting on her bed, idly strumming her guitar. She set it down and calmly opened the door. "Auntie A. Do come in," she said to the fuming duchess.

Amelia stormed into the room, looking in vain for the other two jokesters, but Princess Meredith and Princess Trevi were nowhere in sight. She focused her anger on Tori instead.

"Tori, enough is enough!" she began. "I promised your dear mother that I would raise you to be a proper princess. But now you and your gang of tiny troublemakers have turned a royal occasion into a laughingstock!"

Tori stared at her wide-eyed. "Oh?" she responded as she began to realize how angry her aunt really was. "Don't play the innocent with me!" Duchess Amelia snapped. "This has your mark all over it. I was willing to overlook the exploding cupcakes at the gala and the skunk at the Embassy Ball. I even made excuses when you hid the prime minister's teeth!"

"Just his uppers," Tori corrected her. "Really wish he didn't have that spinach stuck between them."

"Princess Victoria Bethany Evangeline Renée, you are almost eighteen!" cried the duchess. "It's time you started acting like a princess of the realm, not some silly schoolgirl!"

"Forgive me, Aunt Amelia," Tori said, flinching at the sound of her full name. "I'm just having a bit of fun, that's all."

But Duchess Amelia wasn't impressed. "Fun?" she asked. "You're a royal. Duty and responsibility come before fun. Have you even begun to practice your commemoration speech for next week?"

Tori fidgeted. "Um, of course. Okay, sort of. Except for the part after 'Ladies and gentlemen,'" she said.

The duchess threw up her hands, exasperated. "Just as I thought! I'm returning to our guests. And since you refuse to take your duties seriously, you can stay in your room all night and write that speech."

"But Aunt Amelia!" Tori pleaded.

"Not another word!" the duchess said as she turned around and started out the door. Tori grabbed her hairbrush and gave her aunt a hug.

"I am sorry. Good night, Auntie," Tori said.

Her aunt's neat hairdo changed into two wiry braids that stuck straight out on either side of her head. The duchess sighed and stormed out the door, utterly oblivious as her braids nearly slapped against a wall.

Tori giggled to herself. From the other side of the room, a regally groomed Cavalier King

Charles spaniel named Vanessa was watching from a castle-shaped dog bed. She shook her head disapprovingly at Tori.

"Now, really, Vanessa. Don't be so uptight. Even you have to admit it was funny."

Vanessa frowned, then hopped down from her bed and fetched a balled-up piece of paper from a wastebasket. It was Tori's speech. She pushed it toward Tori accusingly.

Tori looked at it and sighed. "Yes, yes, I know, I know. The speech—fine." She began to read from the crinkled piece of paper. "'Ladies and gentlemen, distinguished guests: five hundred years ago, our kingdom began its rule . . . ,' blah, blah, blah. Oh!"

She crumpled the paper up again and threw it back into the wastebasket, then looked wistfully at the Keira poster on her wall. "I'm sorry, Vanessa, but how can I concentrate on a speech when the world's greatest singer is right here in Meribella—and I'm stuck in my room?"

She began to hum one of her favorite Keira songs and was soon singing aloud to Vanessa.

"Look at her
in the spotlight;
I love her purple hair.
She can do
What she wants to,
As crazy as she dares.
She doesn't need to be polite."

Tori picked Vanessa up and began to twirl and dance around the room with her as she sang.

"I wish I had her life.
Then I would be so free.
I wish I had her life—
I'd be another me."

♪

At the same time, Keira was sitting in her dressing room with her guitar, playing random notes. Finally, she gave up in frustration.

"Nothing. Zip. Zero," she said. She set the guitar aside, annoyed at herself. "I don't get it, Riff. Writing songs used to be easy. Used to be fun, even."

Keira turned to see Riff standing on his hind legs, holding a ball in his mouth. She scratched his head and sighed. "But now I'm just drawing a big fat blank."

Riff wagged his tail and brought Keira his rubber hamburger. She petted him, and he immediately rolled over so she could rub his belly. "If only it weren't for all this garbage. Lights, sound, scheduling, payroll, check, double-check—make it work!" she said. "Sometimes I wonder what it would be like to let go."

Then Keira noticed a portrait of the royal family on her dressing room wall. She read the caption engraved on a plaque at the bottom. "Princess Tori. Now, there's a sweet gig. Lives in a castle, has everything done for her. She's probably never worked a day in her life." Keira closed her eyes and imagined what Tori's life must be like. She sang quietly to herself.

"Look at her
in the throne room,
every hair just right.
She has tea in the morning
And bonbons every night.
Wouldn't that be nice?

"I wish I had her life.
Then I would be so free.
I wish I had her life—
I'd be another me."

Chapter 5

While Keira was in her dressing room, Crider was on a video call with Mr. Limburger, his overbearing record company boss.

"Trust me, sir. Keira's new songs are fabulous—best she's ever written!" said Crider. "She just, er, needs a little more time. Of course, I've been helping her as best I can, but you know how these stars are. As a former star myself, I can tell you—"

Mr. Limburger cut him off. "Crider, your job is to keep that little diva in line! You tell her if I don't hear some new hit tunes during that broadcast on Saturday, she can start looking for another record company!"

"B-but, Mr. Limburger—" Crider began.

"And you can go back to managing Uncle

Herman and His Talking Pig!" Mr. Limburger said, and ended the call before Crider could say another word.

"That yappy pig still owes me forty bucks," Crider said bitterly. He tried to stand up, but a wad of chewing gum stretched between his pants and the chair seat. "What the . . . ?" Crider grunted as he tried to get rid of it. The gum wouldn't loosen its hold. Finally, he crossed to the door with the stretched gum pulling the desk chair behind him. He opened the door and yelled, "RU-PERT!"

Backstage, a gum-chewing roadie at the top of a high ladder turned and waved cheerfully. "Right here, Mr. Crider!"

Crider winced as Rupert suddenly lost his balance and fell from the ladder with a crash. But Rupert was at Crider's door in no time, wearing a five-foot section of ladder across his shoulders, his head stuck between two of its rungs. "Something you wanted?" Rupert asked, still smiling.

Crider pointed to the gum stuck between his

chair and his rear end. Rupert was delighted. "Oh, you found it! Thanks!"

"Get. It. Off," said Crider.

Rupert shoved through the doorway, breaking the ladder on both sides. Two rungs still hung around his neck. As he tried to detach the gum from Crider, Crider paced around the room, pulling the desk chair behind him.

"'Keep that little diva in line,'" Crider grumbled as he paced. "How am I supposed to make that whiny warbler do anything? She runs the show like a drill sergeant! Things were different when I was a star.

"Rupert," Crider said wistfully, "do you know I was beloved? I was a beloved idol of millions. The finest boy singer on the *Chipper Chipmunk Show*. Until that tragic day . . ."

Crider thought back to when he had been fourteen, wearing a chipmunk hat and standing before a curtain, singing, when suddenly, his voice cracked. The audience had howled with laughter as Crider turned beet red. He shuddered at the memory. "And that was that," he said. "My singing career was over. To this day I have nightmares of chipmunks, with their toothy smiles, taunting me."

Rupert nodded sympathetically as he finally tore the gum from the seat of Crider's pants. "A tragic tale, Mr. Crider. I get a lump in my throat every time you tell it. Which is quite a bit."

Rupert looked around for a place to put the old gum. He spotted Crider's laptop and stuck the gum on the keyboard. Then he closed it. Crider didn't notice; he was too busy mourning the lost stardom of his youth. "It's all so, so very unfair, Rupert. "If only I had the means to restart my career. All I need is one lucky break, or a rich widow."

Crider resolved to do whatever was necessary to get the money he needed.

Chapter 6

The following day, the royal family was having an afternoon tea for those involved in the Festival. Keira, Crider, and Rupert mingled with the royals. The three princesses were there with King Frederic, but Crider immediately set his sights on Duchess Amelia.

"Oh, Mr. Crider, how you do go on!" Duchess Amelia gushed as Crider showered her with compliments.

"But surely you must have been a ballerina!" Crider insisted. "That form, that grace! I'm certain I saw you dance in *Swan Lake*. Now, don't deny it!"

"You are such a flatterer," the duchess said, blushing. "And you say you were a singer on this *Squeaky Squirrel Show?*"

"Chipmunk. *The Chipper Chipmunk Show*," Crider replied. "But I don't really like to talk about myself," When Rupert, standing nearby, overheard this last bit, he choked in disbelief and sprayed several dignitaries with a mouthful of tea.

On the other side of the room, the handsome young Prince Liam was discussing the state of his kingdom with his elderly uncle, Duke Trentino, and King Frederic.

"I fear this drought has been hard on the entire kingdom. Our reservoirs are only thirty percent full, and our vineyards are withering," Duke Trentino told the king.

Liam glanced past the duke and spotted Tori standing across the room. He smiled at the lovely princess as she extended her hand to the pop star everyone at the Festival was talking about.

♪

Keira was dressed in a short purple dress with a shimmery blue skirt. Her long purple hair was held back with a shiny star headband, and she wore her knee-high purple high-heeled boots. She held out her hand as the royal page introduced her to Princess Tori. "Miss Keira, presenting Her Royal Highness Princess Victoria Bethany Evangeline Renée of Meribella."

"This is so cool!" Tori said excitedly.

"So you're a real, live princess," Keira said. "Awesome." She smiled as a photographer snapped a picture.

"And you're . . . you're Keira! I am absolutely your very biggest fan ever!" Tori said.

"Thanks," Keira replied as she looked around the lavish reception room.

"Would you like a tour?" Tori asked, hoping the pop star would say yes.

"I'd love one! But aren't you supposed to be hostessing or something?" Keira whispered.

"Oh. Right," Tori said, and tapped her finger to her chin thoughtfully. Then she pointed to a window and gasped. "Look, everyone! Robot pandas!" As the guests rushed to the window, Tori grabbed Keira's hand and took off.

Prince Liam was just about to approach the princess and the pop star, but Tori was already pulling a hesitant Keira down the hall.

"Robot pandas?" said Keira with a chuckle. "Where did you come up with that?"

"A lot of practice," said Tori as she pulled Keira up a flight of stairs. "This way. We'll start with my room!"

Chapter 7

Tori led Keira up a grand staircase, then gestured to her room and opened the door. "Ta-da!" she said.

Keira was amazed at all the posters and souvenirs. "Whoa, look at all this. There's more me here than in my house, and I live there!" she said.

"Absolutely," Tori said proudly. "Your guitar, your albums, most of your fashion line."

Keira picked up a funky hat. "I wore this in my first music video," she said.

"It's still my favorite!" Tori said. She sang the opening line of "Here I Am" and did one of Keira's signature dance steps.

Keira smiled. "You even know my moves. Cool. But it's a little more like this," she said.

She set her tote bag down on the floor and began to go over dance steps with Tori.

"Not too shabby for a princess," Keira said as they ended their dance with a flourish. "Hey, want to join me onstage for a number? The tabloids will go nuts. Free publicity."

Tori shook her head. "Thank you. But I'm no performer. Not like you. I'd be freaked to face a real audience. That must be so amazing."

"Sometimes, yeah," Keira replied. "But it's a lot of work. And I've been doing it all my life."

"I read you've been performing since you were six," said Tori.

"Actually, five. And every day since," Keira said wearily. "Plus voice lessons, guitar lessons, dance lessons, recording and concert dates . . ."

"But you love it, right?" Tori asked.

"Sure, it's all I've ever wanted," replied Keira. "But I don't know, it used to be more about the music. Now . . . it's different." Keira bent down to peer inside Tori's castle dollhouse. Behind her, Tori's dog, Vanessa, sniffed Keira's tote bag suspiciously.

"But Keira, you're a *star*!" exclaimed Tori.

"Yeah, and you're a *princess*," said Keira. "When I was little, I dreamed of being a princess!" She twirled around in an imaginary gown. "I'd be wearing a tiara and a ball gown, gliding down a beautiful staircase."

"Care to try mine?" Tori offered Keira her tiara to try on. Keira placed it on her head and posed in front of Tori's full-length mirror, smiling as her fantasy came to life.

"That looks nice," Keira said dreamily.

Suddenly, the girls heard a bark. Keira's puppy, Riff, bounced out of the tote bag, startling Vanessa. Riff began to run happily around the room.

"Sorry!" said Keira. "He's my baby. I bring him everywhere. Riff, sit!"

"He's cute," said Tori. "Look, Vanessa, Keira brought a friend for you."

Vanessa watched Riff warily as Tori adjusted the tiara on Keira's head.

"There," said Tori. "Every girl needs a tiara."

Keira had an idea. "I've got just the outfit

to go with it!" she said. She pulled her magical microphone out of her pocket, then spun around and waved it in the air. "Formal Gown Number Nine!" *Zing!* Keira was suddenly enveloped in a cloud of sparkles and in an instant, she was wearing a gown like Tori's.

"So *that's* how you make those lightning-quick costume changes!" exclaimed Tori. "A magical microphone!"

Keira nodded. "It was passed down to me by my great-aunt Rickie. She rocked the sixties."

"Brilliant! I have something like that," Tori said. She took her hairbrush from her pocket and waved it over her hair. "Pop Whirlwind Number Five!" Tori commanded. A burst of glitter surrounded Tori's head. When the glitter fell away, her hair matched Keira's!

"A magical hairbrush! Very cool," Keira said.

"New hairdos for every royal occasion," said Tori with a smile. "And a few nonroyal ones."

The girls looked at each other's magical devices. "You mind?" they both asked at the same time.

"Pop-Star Daytime Number Sixty-One!" Keira said. She waved her microphone at Tori.

"Royal Princess Number Forty-Three!" said Tori, waving her hairbrush at Keira.

A shimmering cloud surrounded both girls. When it dissolved, Tori was wearing a copy of Keira's party dress, to go with her new Keira hairdo. She even had several chains hanging around her neck to match Keira's. And Keira's hair was in an elegant Tori updo, to go with her new Tori gown. They turned back to the mirror and gasped.

"You look just like me!" Keira and Tori said simultaneously.

Riff and Vanessa looked back and forth between the girls, confused.

"Whoa," Keira said, stunned. Tori giggled.

Just then, Tori's bedroom door swung open and Duchess Amelia barged in. "There you are! The guests are all asking about you! You need to return at once!" She grabbed Keira's hand, thinking she was Tori.

"Oh, no, no," stammered Keira. "I'm—"

"Princess Tori of Meribella!" interrupted Tori. "Your Highness!"

Keira looked at Tori in confusion. Tori smiled sneakily and put a finger to her lips. If they could fool Aunt Amelia, they could fool anyone.

Vanessa and Riff exchanged worried looks as the duchess dragged the "princess" back to the party. But Keira and Tori gave each other a mischievous grin. The game was on.

Chapter 8

Disguised as Princess Tori, Keira descended the top of the grand staircase that led down to the reception hall. The real Tori scurried after her, looking just like Keira.

"Now socialize with your guests!" the duchess told Keira firmly. Then Amelia noticed Crider at the bottom of the stairs. "Yoo-hoo! Oh, Mr. Crider!" she called. She quickly descended the staircase, leaving the two girls to peer down at the assembled guests.

"Well," Tori whispered to Keira, "here's the staircase. Ready for your elegant entrance, Princess?"

Keira stared at the guests. "It's just like I dreamed," she said. "Except I can't move."

"All you need is an introduction," Tori whispered, then made an announcement to the guests. “Her Royal Highness Princess Tori of Meribella—uh, is back.” Tori gave Keira a little nudge. The fake princess gulped, then began to descend the staircase.

At the bottom of the stairs, Prince Liam was chatting with a guest when he saw Keira as Tori coming down the stairs. He was waiting to greet the princess when her shoe caught the hem of her gown and sent her tumbling.

“Whoa!” cried Keira.

Liam leaped up and tried to catch Keira, but the force of her hurtling body knocked them both over. They tumbled to the ground with a crash.

Tori winced as she watched Liam try to help Keira to her feet. “Very elegant,” she said to herself, and zipped down the stairs, hoping to help.

“Are you all right, Your Highness?” Liam asked. “Did you break anything? I mean, besides my toe?”

“I'm good,” Keira replied. “Thanks for almost catching me. Nobody saw that, right?”

"It's our secret," Liam said with a grin.

King Frederic rushed over. "Tori! Tori!"

For a moment, Keira forgot she was posing as the princess. "Who?" she asked blankly. Then she remembered and nodded. "Oh."

"Are you hurt?" the king asked as he hugged her. Keira was in a panic. She had no idea who he was.

"I'm fine. Really. I'm great, Mr., uh . . ."

The real Tori slid in behind her and whispered, "Father."

"Mr. Father," Keira said quickly.

King Frederic smiled. "Thank goodness! You had me worried."

Just then, Princess Meredith joined them. "Keira?" she said. Keira and Tori turned toward her voice.

"Yes?" they both answered at the same time.

Meredith walked up to Tori, thinking she was Keira. Trevi trailed behind her. "I'm a big fan!" said Meredith. "We both are! Not as big as Tori, mind you." Meredith thrust a piece of paper and a pen in front of Tori.

Tori stared blankly at the paper and pen. Then she took them, thinking they were gifts. "Well, er, thank you. What lovely stationery," she said with a smile.

The real Keira leaned in and whispered under her breath, "Autograph."

"Oh! Oh!" Tori said. "Of course! An autograph. Here you go." She signed the paper quickly. Meredith smiled and walked away, but Trevi lingered for a moment, looking at the pop star curiously. Tori shifted uneasily, tapping her finger on her chin.

"Tori, have you met Duke Trentino?" asked King Frederic as the duke joined them.

"Your Highness," the duke said, bowing deeply to the princess. He waited for her to extend her hand, but Keira wasn't sure what she was supposed to do. Finally, she bowed back to him saying, "Your, uh, dukeness."

The duke was puzzled. He bowed lower and said, "An honor."

Keira, still unsure, bowed even lower. "The honor is mine," she said.

Duke Trentino strained as he bowed even lower. "A great privilege," he said.

The king watched in bewilderment as the princess doubled over and said, "A greater privilege."

Across the room, the duchess glanced up from her conversation with Crider and did a double take at the bizarre contortions. Tori sidled over and whispered "Get up" to Keira.

"I don't think I can," Keira said pitifully. With an effort, she stood up straight.

The duke tried to rise, but when he did, his back made a terrible noise, and suddenly he couldn't move at all. Prince Liam helped him to a chair as Keira and Tori made a quick exit to the castle hallway, stifling their laughter.

Chapter 9

The two girls burst out laughing as they walked past suits of armor lining the hall. "I loved your grand entrance! Good thing you didn't crush the poor prince!" Tori said to Keira.

"Hey, he was cute," Keira replied.

"He's the Prince of Stuffingsburg. Forget him. My father says they don't even let women hold office there," said Tori.

"Seriously?" Keira asked, astounded. "In that case, lock him in the tower!"

"Speaking of the tower, would you like to see it?" asked Tori. "We never did finish our tour!"

"Uh . . . ," Keira replied hesitantly. "I'm not really good with heights. How about the ground floor?"

Tori smiled and led Keira down a hallway

lined with portraits of her royal ancestors. "Okay. But actually, you're the princess today, so you should give the tour!"

Keira laughed. "As you wish, Your Highness, or *My* Highness. Or Somebody's Highness. To our left is the Royal Corridor of Creaky Old People."

"Uh-uh," Tori said, correcting her. "You mean Creepy Old People."

They stopped at an ornate wooden wall panel featuring a carving of leaves and flowers surrounding a beautiful gardenia.

"Can you keep a secret?" asked Tori. "A big one?"

"Of course," Keira said.

Tori grinned mischievously. Then she rotated the carved flower clockwise and slid a carved leaf to the left. The wooden panel suddenly swung open, revealing a dark, ancient hallway with a bright light at the far end. "Follow me," Tori said.

Keira gasped when they reached the end of the hall. She was suddenly standing in a strange secret garden filled with bright, colorful blooms, sparkling waterfalls, and fantastic shimmering topiary. Tori led Keira to the center of the room, where a large gardenia plant grew. Each of its blossoms glittered with almond-sized diamonds.

"It's the Diamond Gardenia," explained Tori. "It's five hundred years old, and it grows real diamonds! Most of our people think it's just a legend. Except for the royal family—and now you."

Keira was dazzled. She noticed tiny winged creatures buzzing around the flower. They seemed to be working with miniature gardening tools. One of the creatures landed on Keira's wrist. She looked at it closely and discovered that it was a person with wings! "And the tiny flying people?" she asked.

"They're garden fairies," Tori replied. "They take care of all the plants."

Keira smiled. "They're adorable." Suddenly the room was filled with tiny giggles.

"But they get rather cranky if you mess with the Diamond Gardenia," Tori said. She led

Keira to an ancient mural hanging on one wall of the garden. The mural showed the Diamond Gardenia with its roots extending in every direction. "The legend says that the plant's roots spread all through the kingdom. Without it, Meribella would wither and die."

As Tori spoke, the Diamond Gardenia in the mural seemed to magically fade and wither, causing the rest of the kingdom to fade. "That's why the garden fairies are very protective," she added.

Keira watched the fairies as they tended the gardenia, watering it with tiny watering cans and tilling the soil with miniature hoes. "Awesome," she said, astounded. "What do you guys do with the diamonds?"

"The diamonds help pay for schools, roads, bridges, and other things. They bloom just once every five years, so this is only the third time I've seen it happen," Tori replied.

Just then, Tori noticed that two small diamonds were lying on the ground at the base of the Diamond Gardenia.

"Keira, look!" she said as she bent down and picked them up.

Two of the garden fairies gently took the diamonds from Tori's open palm while other fairies removed two thin chains from her pop-star outfit. The fairies huddled in a corner and buzzed busily.

"What are they doing?" asked Keira.

"I have no idea," said Tori.

The fairies flew back to the girls carrying necklaces they had made by stringing a tiny diamond on each of the chains. They placed one necklace on Tori and one on Keira and giggled.

"They want us to have them!" said Tori.

Keira was delighted. "Hey, thanks, tiny dancers! These rock."

"These will be our friendship necklaces," Tori said excitedly. Then she froze. Her aunt Amelia stood in the doorway to the secret garden.

Chapter 10

"Tori?" Duchess Amelia asked angrily, storming into the garden. "Are you mad, bringing an outsider in here?"

"I—I—" Keira stammered, remembering she was supposed to be Princess Tori.

"You know the rules!" Aunt Amelia shouted. "No one but the royal family is supposed to be in this garden! And you reveal it to a perfect stranger?"

Keira was speechless. But before she could decide what to say, Tori leaped to the rescue. "Now, wait just a minute! You can't talk that way to her in front of a perfect stranger. If the princess could speak, which she can't, because she's, er, speechless, she would say that you're being way too strict!"

While the bewildered duchess tried to sort out that protest, Tori grabbed Keira's hand and made a hasty exit.

Meanwhile, Crider, who had been hiding behind a stone column in the hall, saw the two girls run past him. He peered around the column and saw the Diamond Gardenia through the open door to the garden. Dazzled by all the diamonds, he gasped.

When the duchess came back into the hall, Crider quickly retreated. Peeking around a corner, he watched as the duchess shut the secret panel and carefully moved the pieces of the wooden gardenia back into place.

Crider jotted the moves down on a small piece of paper. Then he rushed back to the Great Hall and tried to look casual when the duchess returned. "Problem, my dear?" he asked her.

Duchess Amelia shook her head. "You wouldn't believe it. Now, where were we with our tour?"

In Tori's room, the two girls leaned against the closed door, doubled over with laughter. Their dogs jumped up and down, barking for attention.

"Whew! That was close!" Tori said, gasping. "I thought she'd ground us both!"

"Look, Princess, your secret's safe with me, honest," Keira said, collapsing into a chair.

Tori nodded. "I'm certain of it. You seem like a real friend."

"Well, thanks," Keira replied. "For a princess, you're a lot of fun." They both petted their dogs as Keira continued. "Between touring and recording, I don't get much time for fun—or friends."

"So, friends forever?" Tori asked.

Keira nodded. "Friends forever." As the two girls grinned, their necklaces sparkled magically. "But if you don't mind, Princess Victoria, I'd—"

"Please—call me Tori."

Keira smiled. "Tori. Got it. Look, this was awesome, but I've got a tour to obsess over, so let's change back before we get in more trouble."

"Why does it have to end?" Tori asked. "Why can't we keep on being each other?"

"Well, for one thing," said Keira, "I've got a concert to do tonight. Not to mention contracts to sign, an interview—"

Tori was too excited to take no for an answer. "But what about tomorrow? We could change places in the morning and spend the whole day being each other!"

Keira still wasn't convinced. "Look, I really don't think—"

"Keira, wouldn't it be amazing—just for one day—to take a break from being you?" asked Tori.

"I'd get to be a pop star for a whole day. And you'd get to be a princess! It'd be just like in your dream!"

Tori smiled as Keira slowly began to change her mind. . . .

Chapter 11

Early the next morning, Tori and Keira were in the castle reception hall, surrounded by a cloud of sparkles. When the sparkles cleared, the girls stood opposite each other at the top of the sweeping staircase. Tori looked just like Keira, and Keira looked just like Tori.

"Tell me again—why did I let you talk me into this?" Keira asked as Vanessa and Riff played at their feet.

"Because you really, really want to do it! And more importantly, because I really, really want to do it!" Tori replied happily.

As the girls sat on a satin sofa, Keira showed Tori pictures on her smartphone. "Okay, look," Keira explained. "If you're going to be me today, you should know that the stage manager's name is Nora and the choreographer's is Daniel. We've got rehearsals this morning."

"No problem!" Tori said enthusiastically. "I know all your songs and dance moves by heart. Oh, I'd better give you your princess schedule for today." She pulled out a paper scroll and read from it. "Let's see. There's breakfast on the terrace, then you judge the flower show at ten and christen a yacht at eleven. . . . There's a luncheon at the Milvanian embassy—"

"Flower show? Embassy? Yacht?" Keira asked in astonishment.

"It's easy!" replied Tori. She began to sing.

"To be a princess is to know
which spoon to use.
To be a princess is
a thousand pairs of shoes!

"Have your breakfast
served in bed.
Wear some diamonds
on your head.

"Get a foot massage
and mani-pedi, too.
To be a princess is
to live a dream come true."

Soon, Keira jumped in to show Tori how to be a pop star.

"To be a pop star is to know
which mic to use.
To be a pop star is to not
fall off your shoes.

"To rehearse until it's right,
give a great show every night,
and have room service
with anything you choose.

"To be a pop star is
to love your great reviews."

"Vanessa will help you, and I'll take Riff," said Tori when they were done showing each other what to do. The girls traded dogs and shook hands. "Ready?" Tori asked.

"Ready," Keira declared. The princess and the pop star headed off in opposite directions.

♪

A little while later, Keira sat on the castle terrace, ringing a tiny silver bell. She was soon served a luxurious breakfast at a beautifully laid table. Vanessa sat across from her on a velvet cushion, eating from a crystal dish.

A servant entered with a silver-domed serving platter. He bowed as he removed the lid to reveal a watermelon that had been carved into the shape of a swan. It was filled with a fancy fruit salad. Keira waved it away unenthusiastically, and the servant immediately replaced it with an enormous ice cream sundae. Keira smiled and clapped delightedly.

When Keira reached for her soup spoon, Vanessa barked. Keira looked up to see Vanessa shaking her head. Keira gestured tentatively to the dessert spoon and Vanessa nodded. Keira smiled, picked up the correct spoon, and dug in!

After breakfast, Keira floated out the castle's front entrance with Vanessa on a jeweled leash. Palace guards on both sides of the walkway bowed deeply as she passed. "I could stay this way forever," Keira thought as she headed toward a waiting horse-drawn carriage.

A palace guard opened the carriage door and said, "Your Highness." Keira stopped. She took a step back and leaned over to the guard. He bowed again and said, "Your Highness." Keira giggled. She loved being called that. "It just never gets old," she said as she gracefully glided into the waiting carriage, which took her to judge the kingdom's flower show.

The garden club members applauded politely as Keira smiled and placed a blue ribbon on a potted dahlia held by its proud owner, Lady Hamilton. But when Keira leaned over to smell the winning dahlia, she sneezed, blowing all the petals off the flower. Lady Hamilton looked at her blue-ribboned, bare-stemmed plant in horror.

Keira took it all in stride, however, and was soon walking Vanessa down a red-carpeted marina dock. A servant walked in front of her, strewing flower petals in her path, and bowing dignitaries flanked her on either side. At the end of the dock, Keira stopped at the bow of a yacht, where a dignitary handed her a beribboned champagne bottle. Keira looked blankly at the bottle, uncertain what to do. She suddenly heard a yip and looked down to see Vanessa holding a long twig in her mouth. Keira watched as Vanessa whapped the twig against a mooring post and broke it.

Keira held up the bottle and looked at Vanessa as if to say, "Really?"

Vanessa nodded, and Keira smashed the bottle against the bow of the yacht. The crowd applauded as Keira picked Vanessa up and gave her a big kiss.

Chapter 12

On the amphitheater stage, Tori was thrilled to be at her first rehearsal as a pop star. She was singing Keira's song about a perfect day and loving it. Joined by Keira's backup dancers and supervised by Daniel the choreographer, the disguised princess was keeping up with the steps.

When she was having trouble with one particular step, Tori heard a yip at her feet. She looked down to see Riff standing in front of her, doing the dance moves. She watched him and repeated the step, then gave him a big thumbs-up and a grin.

Later, Tori was backstage, surrounded by adoring Keira fans who were thrusting autograph books at her. She happily signed them all, then

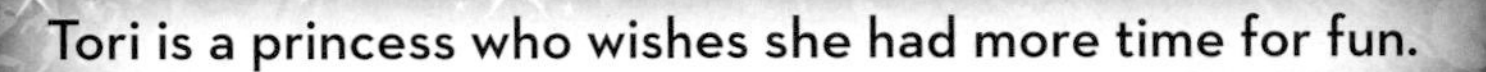

Tori is a princess who wishes she had more time for fun.

Keira is a famous pop star with a very busy schedule.

Tori and Keira meet and become friends right away.

Tori and Keira use their magical devices to make themselves look like each other!

The girls visit the Diamond Gardenia and get special diamond friendship necklaces.

Tori and Keira decide to switch places!

Tori has a perfect pop star day!

Keira has a perfect princess day!

Tori finds out that being a pop star is harder than it seems.

Keira has a hard time acting like royalty.

Tori promises the children in her kingdom a free concert by Keira.

Oh, no! Keira's greedy manager, Crider, steals the Diamond Gardenia.

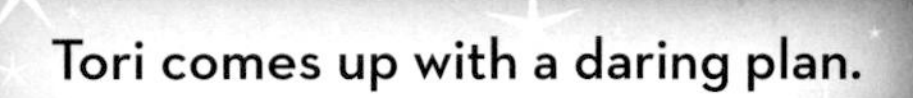

Tori comes up with a daring plan.

Tori and Keira stop Crider!

The girls' friendship necklaces bloom into a new Diamond Gardenia!

Tori and Keira put on the best show the kingdom of Meribella has ever seen.

held each book down so Riff could add his paw print. She posed in front of a stretch limo for hordes of paparazzi. But she wasn't used to all the flashing lights. When she blindly headed off in the wrong direction, Riff led her right to her dressing room. Tori twirled delightedly in front of a vanity as she tried on sparkling eye shadows, blushes, and lipsticks fit for a pop star. Riff ran happily around her.

♪

In Crider's office, Rupert was fixing a stuck drawer on his boss's desk with a screwdriver while Crider paced the room, deep in thought. "You should have seen those diamonds, Rupert! Hundreds of them, just sitting there, glittering!"

But Rupert had his headphones on. "Me, I don't hold with littering," he said.

Crider stretched Rupert's headphones apart, then let go so they snapped back on Rupert's head. "Ow!" Rupert cried.

"Glittering, not littering, you baboon!"

Crider snapped. "Would you please listen? With those diamonds, I could afford to create a stage show that would make me a star again, put me back in the spotlight. And it would finally chase that grinning chipmunk out of my dreams. There must be a way!"

♪

Exhilarated after her fabulous day, Tori exited the backstage door and headed to a waiting limo with Riff. Suddenly, she was intercepted by Nora, who was holding two drawings of headpiece designs. "Keira! You never said which one you want for the 'Smoke and Mirrors' number."

Tori looked at both drawings and grinned. "Oh, I don't know," she said cheerfully. "You choose. Surprise me!" Nora was stunned. Keira never let her make decisions.

Tori continued to walk toward the limo. When she reached it, she knocked on the tinted window and said to the driver, "You know what? I think I'll take Riff for a walk. You go ahead.

“Come on, Riff,” Tori said as they strolled off. “I can’t remember the last time I simply strolled through Meribella.”

Tori and Riff wandered down a country lane. Tori looked around and saw dried-up vineyards and farmland. The houses they passed had fallen into disrepair.

“Huh,” said Tori. “I don’t remember ever being around *here* before, Riff.”

Tori spotted two girls playing hopscotch. “Excuse me!” she called as she approached the girls. “Can you tell me the way back to the marina?”

One of the girls, whose name was Emily, looked at her in surprise.

“Hey, you’re Keira!” She turned to her friend. “Look, Charlotte! *Keira!*”

“Awesome!” Charlotte replied. “Keira, can you sign my T-shirt? I really, really wanted to see your concert!” She held out the bottom of her shirt for the pop star to sign.

Tori smiled. “Well, I’m playing one more show, tomorrow night. Maybe you can see it!”

"I wish!" Charlotte said. "But my dad said we can't afford it."

"Mine too," Emily added. "Bummer, huh?"

Charlotte nodded. "Lots of folks can't afford stuff right now. You know, since the big drought."

Tori was surprised. "Drought?" she asked. "Is that still going on?"

"Oh, yeah. It wiped out all the vineyards this year," Emily told her. "Dad says everyone's struggling to get by."

"I . . . I didn't know," Tori said sadly.

"Well, I guess you'd have to live in Meribella to know about it," Charlotte said. She didn't realize she was talking to the Princess of Meribella.

"Yes, I guess you would," Tori said. She wondered how she couldn't have known something so important about her own people.

Chapter 13

Meanwhile, Crider and Rupert were waiting to see Duchess Amelia at Meribella Castle.

"Mr. Crider! How lovely it is to see you again," said the duchess as she descended the reception room's grand staircase.

Crider carried a stack of drawings, and Rupert had a camera slung around his neck.

"My dear duchess, has it been only a day or an eternity?" Crider asked, and kissed her hand. "Thank you for agreeing to meet me on such short notice. You remember my associate."

The bubble Rupert was blowing with his gum suddenly popped. "Pleased to meet you, I'm sure," Rupert said, and curtsied.

Crider glared at him. Rupert quickly pulled a piece of paper from his pocket, wrapped the gum in it, and crammed the paper back into his pocket. The duchess ignored Rupert and coyly took Crider's arm. "So, Mr. Crider, is there something I can do for you?" she asked, batting her eyelashes.

"I simply thought we should coordinate the details for Saturday's gala. And while you and I talk, I wonder if my associate could take a few snapshots of the palace for our, uh, memory book?" Crider replied, pointing to Rupert.

Duchess Amelia tightened her grip on Crider's arm. "How charming. So it'll be just us."

Crider nodded. "Just us two." Then he turned to Rupert and whispered, "Go to it, Rupert. And please make it snappy."

Rupert wandered down the hallway looking to his left, then his right. "Gardenia panel?" he said to himself, remembering Crider's instructions. "Wonder what a gardenia looks like."

He spotted a door with some carvings on it. He shrugged and went in, stumbling over a mop and a broom.

"Nope, not it," Rupert said as he pulled his

foot out of a pail. He rounded a corner and suddenly found himself face to face with the gardenia panel. "Now, that's a gardenia if I ever saw one!" said Rupert with excitement. "Let's see how Mr. Crider says to open it."

He reached into his pocket and pulled out a crumpled piece of paper. When he opened it, he saw Crider's instructions covered with his discarded piece of gum. "Uh-oh," Rupert said as tried unsticking the gum so he could read Crider's words. "Turn flower. Then push something. Hmm."

Rupert tossed the note away and approached the door. He would give it a go on his own. He rotated the carved flower, but nothing happened. He pushed on the door, but it wouldn't budge.

Then he noticed the suits of armor lining the hallway. One was holding a battle-axe. "Brilliant!"

Rupert took the battle-axe from the suit of armor and stepped over to the door. He swung the axe back and took a mighty whack at the panel. He accidentally chopped through a heavy chain hanging in front of it. *Crash!* A massive medieval chandelier landed on top of him. Shakily, he got to his feet just in time for the rest of the chain to fall and hit him on the head.

♪

While Rupert was struggling with the door, Crider and the duchess were having tea out on the terrace. Crider was showing her his various drawings. "Now, when the royal family arrives at the concert, our band will play your national anthem."

The duchess smiled coyly and scooted her chair closer to Crider's. Crider scooted his a little farther away. The duchess continued to scoot around after Crider.

"You were saying?" she said as she leaned in, batting her eyelashes.

Crider quickly knocked over his tea, which splashed into Amelia's lap. "Ahh!" she yelled as she jumped up and shook out her skirt.

"Oh, now look, I've done it again. I'm just

such a butterfingers," said Crider.

Duchess Amelia smiled and gritted her teeth. "Oh, think nothing of it. I'll just clean this off," she said, and left the room.

"Take your time!" he called after her. Then he looked at his watch impatiently, hoping for Rupert to return with news about the secret gardenia door.

Chapter 14

Still reeling from his tangle with the medieval chandelier, Rupert picked up a crowbar from one of the nearby suits of armor and tried to pry the door open. It still wouldn't budge. In frustration, he hurled the crowbar at the door. It hit the carved leaf, and the door swung open.

"Ka-ching!" Rupert cried as he entered the secret garden. Just as Rupert spotted the Diamond Gardenia, a swarm of angry garden fairies buzzed at his head.

"Shoo! Shoo! Get away!" Rupert hollered, swatting at the fairies. But they kept up the attack, some flying into his sleeves and pant legs and down his shirt. He started to wriggle and squirm, laughing uncontrollably. "No! No! Tickles! Stop it!"

As he wriggled wildly, the little fairies fell out and landed in a heap. Rupert quickly grabbed an empty urn and plopped it over the fairies. Cackling to himself, he took hold of the Diamond Gardenia and shook it hard. All the diamonds fell off the plant, and he gleefully scooped them up and stuffed them in his pockets. He was too excited to notice the urn slowly moving until it finally tipped over with a crash.

Suddenly, Rupert was being attacked by a swarm of dive-bombing fairies. They flew into his ears and pulled his hair.

On the ground, three fairies formed a slingshot out of a forked twig and a vine and shot berries at his head. Two others stretched a garden hose across his path. As he tried to scramble to safety, he tripped and fell to the ground with a thud.

Fairies began to wrap his legs with garden tape, but Rupert grabbed some garden shears and snipped his way out. He dashed out of the garden and slammed the door shut. The fairies were unable to stop him.

♪

As the sun set over the ocean, the lights of Meribella started to blink on. In Keira's dressing room at the amphitheater, Tori was rubbing her tired feet after her long walk and talking to Keira on her cell phone.

Keira laughed as she told Tori about her day. "And then I sneezed every last petal off that lady's flower! Who knew I was allergic to dahlias?"

Tori laughed, too. "And I must have tried every single one of your new eye shadows! Poor Nora is convinced you've gone stark-raving mad!"

"Yeah, by the way, your aunt Amelia is all up in my face about practicing some speech," added Keira.

"The dreaded commemoration speech." Tori rolled her eyes. "I don't suppose you'd like to give it? And by give it, I also mean write it."

"Only if I can sing it," replied Keira. "This has been the coolest day I've had in forever."

"Me too!" agreed Tori. "And I'm certain I've learned more about my kingdom today than I have in my entire seventeen years."

"Too bad the day is over," said Keira. "Unless you want to keep it going one more day?"

"You're on!" Tori said.

"Great!" Keira said excitedly. "The live broadcast is tomorrow, so we'll need to change back early."

"Of course," Tori replied. "I only wish more of my people could afford to go. Seems they're a lot worse off than I knew."

"Well, how about we make the last concert a free one?" suggested Keira. "I'll work out the details."

Tori was thrilled. "Thank you so much!"

"Hey, it's the least a princess can do. See you tomorrow!"

Chapter 15

The next morning, the palace guards raised Meribella's flag. At its center was a lovely white gardenia. Spanning the main street was a decorative arch of gardenias with a banner that read MERIBELLA FESTIVAL 500. Shop windows were covered with garlands of gardenias and posters proclaming MERIBELLA'S 500TH ANNIVERSARY—GALA CELEBRATION AND CONCERT TONIGHT!

The castle was lavishly decorated as well. Strands of lights fanned out from posts surrounding the castle, high on a cliff's edge, and leading all the way down to the marina, hundreds of feet below. The amphitheater and its royal box were also draped in white gardenias. Everything was ready for the day's festivities.

Inside the castle's Great Hall, King Frederic

and Duchess Amelia chatted with Duke Trentino and Prince Liam. The king saw Keira enter as Princess Tori.

"Ah, Tori! You remember Prince Liam and Duke Trentino. They'll be joining us in the royal box tonight."

The duke clicked his heels and bowed, kissing Keira's hand. Liam did the same, with a boyish grin. "Of course. I can truly say that the moment I met your daughter, I fell," Liam said.

Keira grinned. "Nice bumping into you, too."

"Tori will be giving the commemoration speech this week," King Frederic said. "We're very proud of her."

"Really. How very modern of Your Majesty," the duke remarked.

Keira looked at him and arched an eyebrow. "Modern? What do you mean, 'modern'?"

The duchess placed a warning hand on Keira's arm. "Simply a figure of speech, Your Highness," she said.

The duke nodded and smiled. "I was merely complimenting His Majesty for allowing a woman to speak publicly in the name of the kingdom. Most unique."

Keira narrowed her eyes. "Oh, yeah. You guys are from Stuffingsburg, right? You're the ones who still don't let women hold office. Kind of medieval, don't you think? Or is that your idea of 'unique'?"

"Princess Tori!" Duchess Amelia snapped. "That was quite rude. Apologize at once!"

"I'd love to, but it wouldn't mean much, coming from an itty-bitty girl like me," said Keira.

The outraged duke turned to the king. "Your Majesty, I'm afraid we will NOT be able to attend the concert tonight! And our king shall hear about this. Good day!"

As the duke stormed out, Liam turned to Keira. "It's we who should be apologizing," he said. "You're absolutely right. I've been trying for ages to convince my father of the same thing. Don't worry; I'll smooth things over with the duke." Keira smiled, surprised and intrigued by the prince.

When Liam and the duke had left the Great

Hall, Duchess Amelia turned angrily to Keira. "Tori, have you gone mad? It's your new friend, that 'Keira' creature. She's turned you into someone I don't even recognize!"

King Frederic placed a hand on the duchess's arm. "Calm down, Amelia. I've wanted to say the same thing to that pompous windbag for years."

Duchess Amelia bristled. "Frederic, this is really too much to bear! All you do is indulge her! Well, I wash my hands of it!"

As the duchess stormed out, the king put an arm around Keira and shook his head. "She'll get over it," he said calmly. "We'll talk later. First, I have a few things to take care of. The fairies sent some kind of alert from the garden."

Chapter 16

After her encounter with the duke, Keira decided to return to Tori's room for a bit. When she opened the door, she found Trevi and Meredith playing a game.

"Tori! Come play!" called Meredith.

"Oh, no, that's okay. You guys are having fun," Keira said, but Meredith grabbed her hand and pulled her into the room.

"C'mon! You're it!" Trevi cried.

"But I don't really know how to play this game," said Keira.

Meredith handed Keira a blindfold. "You've played it a zillion times! Just try to find us!" she said. Keira reluctantly put on the blindfold.

The little girls shrieked and dodged as Keira felt around for them. Then Keira fell over an ottoman and the girls doubled over in laughter. Keira giggled right along with them before finally grabbing Trevi and shouting, "Gotcha!" Trevi shrieked, and all three girls collapsed on the bed in a giggling heap.

Keira whipped off her blindfold. "That was awesome! But we'd better get ready for tonight."

"Okay," Meredith replied, "but if you're going to keep pretending to be Tori, you'll have to learn to play games the way she does."

Keira looked at them, stunned. "You know?" she finally asked.

"Of course," Trevi said. "If you were Tori, you would have cheated by now."

Meredith laughed, happy to be in on the secret. "It's okay. We won't tell."

Keira grinned just as Trevi hit her from behind with a pillow. *WHAP!* Meredith attacked with another, and the room erupted in giddy laughter as Meredith and Trevi began jumping on the bed.

"Look how high we can fly!" Trevi said joyfully.

Keira suddenly stopped, struck by what Trevi had said.

"'Look how high we can fly,'" she repeated as she picked up Tori's guitar, humming. She plinked a few strings and began singing a new tune. "Look how high we can fly, we can almost touch the sky."

She quickly jotted something on a scrap of paper, then resumed singing and playing.

"Look how high we can fly!
We can see everything
From up here in the sky.
We've got the perfect view
Together, me and you.
Look how high we can fly."

When she ended the song, the sisters applauded enthusiastically. Keira grinned and bowed playfully to them.

Just then, the king entered the room with a serious expression on his face.

"Tori? A moment, please?" he asked.

Keira pursed her lips and looked at the two girls. "Uh-oh. What'd I do now?" she said. She stashed the paper with the new song in her pocket and stepped out into the hall. The king looked terribly distressed.

"Tori, our diamonds have been stolen," he announced.

"Wh-what?" Keira exclaimed.

King Frederic placed a hand on Keira's shoulder. "I don't usually like to bother you with our kingdom's finances. I know it's never been a big interest of yours, but I'm afraid this affects all of us." He sat on a hall chair and put his head in his hands. Keira sat down next to him.

"After the drought," the king continued, "I was counting on the new diamond harvest to help Meribella through this hard time. But now I don't know how I'll feed our people."

"Don't worry, Dad," Keira said. "We'll find out who did this and get those diamonds back, I promise." She stood up and took on the resolute determination she was used to having as a pop star. "We can start by checking security to see who was in the castle. I'll handle everything. But first, there's someone I've got to call!"

Chapter 17

At the amphitheater, Tori was onstage for a rehearsal with Daniel, the choreographer, and the whole company of dancers.

"I want to make a change," said Daniel. "Let's work on that new move you showed me. You remember."

Riff's ears suddenly went up. "I do?" Tori asked nervously.

Daniel clapped his hands. "Ready? And . . . five, six, seven, eight!"

As the dancers began the routine, Tori desperately tried to follow the moves, but she was two beats behind, bumping and crashing into everyone. It wasn't long before she was sprawled out on the stage. She'd somehow managed to topple the scenery and the TV camera equipment before hitting the floor.

"Well, that was an interesting new step," Daniel said sarcastically.

Tori looked around at the damage. "Sorry—really, I am. And I'm sorry about the camera. And the amp. And the spotlight."

"Let's just go back to the moves you remember," Daniel said wearily. "It's safer for the rest of us."

Tori smiled sheepishly as Daniel helped her up. She didn't notice that her cell phone fell out of her pocket next to the amps.

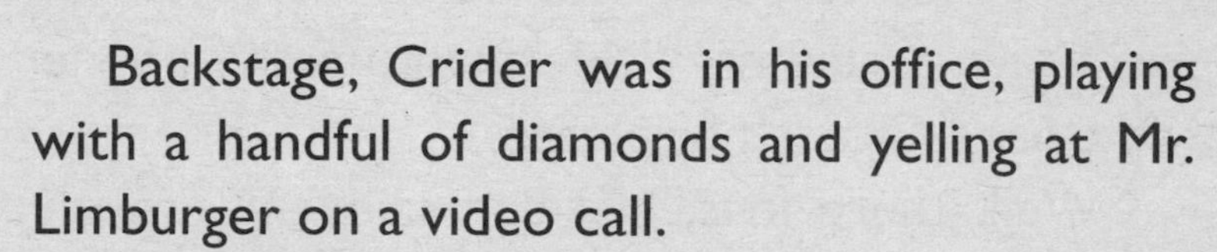

Backstage, Crider was in his office, playing with a handful of diamonds and yelling at Mr. Limburger on a video call.

"I'm through with you—and on to stardom!" said Crider. "I'm taking off! You can handle this broadcast yourself!"

Crider slammed his laptop closed and did a gleeful little dance. "How I love show business!"

Rupert nodded as he packed Crider's

briefcase with pictures and papers. "You mean you're not going to stay for the show tonight?" he asked.

"You can stay if you want," replied Crider. "But I've had it with playing nursemaid to that diva. I've got a new career to launch!" He let a handful of diamonds fall like rain into a clear plastic bag. "With these babies, I'm back! Picture it, Rupert, up there in lights: *Crider! The Legend Returns!*" Crider's phone suddenly rang. He glanced at the caller ID and growled, "The duchess again! Tell her I'm busy!"

Rupert picked up the phone. "Hello? Sorry, Your Grace, he's busy not being interested in you. Have a nice day!" He hung up the phone and closed Crider's briefcase.

"Well, there it is," Crider said. "We're on our way. And for your invaluable services, I'm offering you the same job you have now. And at the same pay!"

"Dreams really do come true . . . all thanks to a few sparklies. Imagine if we had the whole plant," Rupert said, and blew a large bubble.

Crider dropped his briefcase and his eyes grew wide as saucers. "Rupert, you're a genius! We've been thinking too small. Why just settle for a few diamonds? Tonight we go back and grab that plant!"

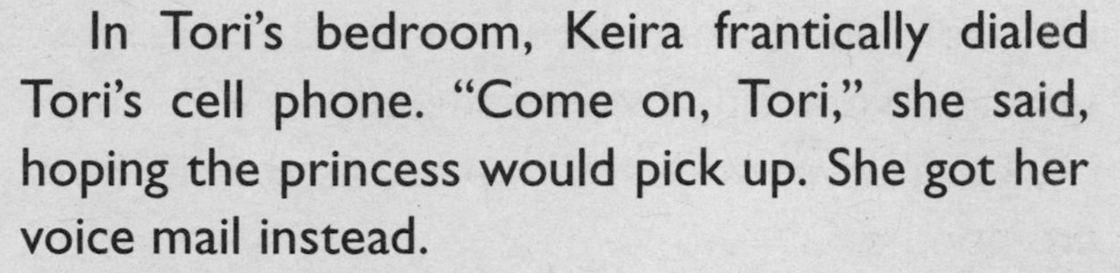

In Tori's bedroom, Keira frantically dialed Tori's cell phone. "Come on, Tori," she said, hoping the princess would pick up. She got her voice mail instead.

"Tori, this is Keira. I'm on my way over. Something's happened and we need to talk. Call me when you get this!" Keira hung up and grabbed Vanessa. As she approached the bedroom door, she heard the lock click. She reached for the knob, but it wouldn't turn.

Keira pounded on the door. "Hey!" she cried. "What's going on? Let me out!"

"Not until you've learned some manners, young lady!" replied the duchess from the hallway. "Your treatment of our guests today was inexcusable! And you still have to write your speech!"

"No, no—you don't understand!" Keira yelled frantically through the door. "I've got to get to the concert! Look, I'm not the princess! I'm Keira!"

"Of all the preposterous excuses!" the duchess said with a laugh. "Well, it's too late for more of your pranks! You'll stay in there tonight until you've finished your speech!"

Keira's eyes widened in panic as the duchess stomped off.

Chapter 18

At the amphitheater, the strings of lights leading from the castle down to the marina flickered to life. The arch of the amphitheater was aglow with a neon sign reading MERIBELLA FESTIVAL 500, decorated with large neon gardenias. The excited crowd filed in for the concert.

The king stepped from a horse-drawn royal carriage onto a red carpet, followed by princesses Meredith and Trevi and the duchess. The royal party entered the royal box, where Prince Liam and Duke Trentino stood to greet them. Liam had convinced the duke to attend after all.

"Your Majesty," said the duke and the prince in unison. The king smiled only slightly. He was still worried about the castle theft, but as king he had to attend the Festival. The audience stood respectfully as the Meribellan national anthem played. The royals waved, then took their seats. Liam looked at the empty chair next to the little girls, disappointed. He scanned the area for any sign of Princess Tori.

Backstage, Tori was in costume and ready for the opening number, but she was panicking. Four dancers fussed around her, touching up her makeup, hair, and outfit.

Nora peeked her head in the door, wearing her stage manager's headset. "Ten minutes to curtain! And Mr. Limburger's here to supervise the broadcast."

When Nora and the dancers left, Tori paced back and forth in the dressing room. Curled up in a corner, Riff watched her from his dog bed. "Where is she, Riff?" asked Tori. "Something's wrong. Keira would never miss her show. And where did my phone go?" She couldn't find it in her pockets or her purse.

"Nine minutes!" Nora shouted.

Tori was suddenly terrified. "I can't do this!" she said.

A few minutes later, the band started to play the intro to Keira's opening number. Tori paced.

Soon Nora banged on the door. "Keira, where are you? You're on in thirty seconds!"

"No, you don't understand!" cried Tori. "I can't! I'm no performer!"

"What are you talking about?" asked Nora. "Keira, some of those people have been waiting hours to see you! It's your responsibility to give them a show!"

As the words sank in, Tori looked at the closed-circuit monitor, which was panning the expectant crowd. She saw Emily and Charlotte from the run-down farmhouses seated in the front row, waiting excitedly.

"Keira, please get out there!" yelled Nora. "Limburger's having a fit. That guy can destroy your career!"

Tori closed her eyes. "Keira's career," she whispered to herself.

A moment later, Tori opened the dressing room door. "I'm ready," she said quietly.

♪

"Come on, Tori," said Keira. She was sitting in Tori's locked bedroom, dialing the princess's number over and over again. As she hung up in frustration, she heard a car outside the window. She looked down to see her limo pulling up to the castle entrance. Rupert and Crider stepped out and walked to the castle's main door. "What are they doing here?" she wondered aloud.

Keira went to the door and banged on it again, but it was useless. Suddenly, Vanessa began to bark.

"Quiet, Vanessa, please. I'm trying to think. There's just got to be a way out of here."

Keira heard the band play the intro to her first number at the amphitheater. It was followed by silence. She knew something had to be terribly wrong.

Vanessa began to tug at Keira's gown, pulling

her across the room. When they reached the spot where Tori's secret panel was located, Vanessa stopped and scratched at the wall.

Keira caught on. "Push?" she asked, and pressed against the wall panel. The panel slid open to reveal a secret tunnel. Keira was stunned. "Vanessa, why didn't you tell me?"

Vanessa rolled her eyes as Keira followed her through the tunnel to another secret panel that led into the castle's reception room.

"Good girl!" Keira said to Vanessa. "Now let's get out of here!"

♪

Outside the palace, Crider and Rupert approached the guards flanking the entrance. "We won't be a minute. The duchess sent me back to fetch her spectacles. You know how she is," said Crider with a wink.

"Yes, sir, Mr. Crider," the guard replied.

The guard opened the castle door, and Crider entered with Rupert following behind him.

Chapter 19

At the amphitheater, the audience waited uneasily, confused by the long delay. A hush settled over the crowd when Tori finally walked onstage as Keira. She was holding an acoustic guitar. Tori turned toward the audience, terrified. She opened her mouth to sing, but all that came out was a squeak.

Tori turned to the band, which again had started to play Keira's loud opening intro. "Sorry," she told them. "I only know how to do this alone." The band stopped playing.

Then Tori turned back to the audience and quietly began to sing Keira's opening song, "Here I Am," with only her acoustic guitar for accompaniment.

"When I was young,
I played for fun;
Made up the words
Nobody heard.

"But now I see
All eyes on me
And suddenly,
I'm in a dream.

"I got a feeling now
Everything's right somehow.

"Here I am,
Being who I want,
Giving what I got.
Never a doubt now.

"Here I go,
Burning like a spark,
Light up the dark
Again."

The audience and the band were stunned, and then completely entranced.

As Tori sang and she began to feel more comfortable onstage, her voice grew stronger and livelier. Soon the band joined in, and the backup singers and dancers tried to keep up with Tori as she rocked out on her own version of "Here I Am." The crowd cheered and whistled, swaying to the music.

"There's a star that's right inside you,
So come and let it out,
Find out what you're about and just shout.

"Here I am,
Being who I want,
Giving what I got.
Never a doubt now.

"Here I go,
Burning like a spark,
Light up the dark
Again."

Tori had the audience in the palm of her hand. "Hello, Meribella!" she shouted. "I never dreamed I'd be up here in such an awesome kingdom!"

She looked out to where Trevi and Meredith were sitting with the king and the duchess in the audience. "You have the coolest princesses in the universe!" The crowd cheered, and Trevi and Meredith beamed. "In fact, Tori told me she's committed to doing everything she can to help everyone, especially those who are less fortunate." The king shared a surprised look with the duchess as the audience burst into applause.

♪

At the palace, Crider and Rupert found the door of the secret garden. They both wore beekeeper hats and veils to keep the garden fairies at bay.

"I don't see those dive-bombin' pixies," Rupert said as they stepped into the garden. Suddenly, a furious swarm of garden fairies attacked. Crider ducked, swatting them away, but the fairies lifted off his hat and swooped down on him mercilessly.

Rupert reached into his coat and pulled out an aerosol can. "Brought some bug spray just in case!" Rupert aimed the can at Crider and the fairies and sprayed.

"That's not bug spray!" Crider said, coughing. "It's hair spray!"

But to Rupert's delight, the spray made the fairies' wings stick together. They plummeted to the ground in an angry heap. Rupert smiled. "Well, anyway, it did the job."

Crider looked at the Gardenia plant, stripped of its diamonds from Rupert's previous visit. "Grab the plant!" he growled.

Rupert found a mini hand trowel and started to dig around at the base of the plant while Crider grabbed the stem and tugged. But the plant wouldn't budge. "These roots must go deep. Dig deeper!" Crider said to Rupert.

As Rupert dug and Crider pulled even harder, the lights in the garden started to flicker. All around the kingdom, lights dimmed. Flowers wilted, trees dropped their leaves, and the garden's sparkling waterfall slowly dried to a trickle.

Crider and Rupert tugged at the Gardenia plant, but the roots seemed to go on forever. Finally, Crider lost his patience. He grabbed a pair of gardening shears and began to snip at the plant's roots. With one huge tug, the thieves eventually yanked the plant out of the soil and stuffed it into a burlap bag.

"Now let's get down to the boat!" Crider said triumphantly. As they ran out of the castle, the gardenia's branches began to droop.

Chapter 20

Onstage, Tori was bowing to thunderous applause when she noticed the lights of the kingdom dim and flicker. She looked out at the landscaping around the theater. All the flowers seemed to have died, and the trees were losing their leaves. Tori gasped. "The Diamond Gardenia!" she thought. She stepped forward and addressed the audience. "Uh, and now a brief intermission!" Then she ran off the stage and out of the amphitheater.

Tori looked around frantically for some sort of transportation. She spotted the horse-drawn carriage the royal family had arrived in. "Perfect," Tori said as she ran up to the driver. "Sergeant! To the castle! Right away!"

But Tori still looked like Keira. The driver

looked at her in confusion. "I'm sorry, miss," he said politely, "but this carriage is for the royal family only."

"But I am the royal—" Tori began, and stopped before revealing her secret. "Oh. Of course. Hang on." She pulled out her hairbrush, and after it released a cloud of sparkles, the princess's blond hair was back. She looked like Tori again, but she was still wearing Keira's stage costume. "There. Now, to the castle!" she said to the driver.

"I don't know," said the driver, bewildered by her sudden transformation. "I'd better check with His Majesty."

As the driver ran off, Tori jumped into the carriage and took the reins. "Fine! I'll drive it myself!" she said.

"Wait! I'm coming with you!" Tori spun around to see Prince Liam running toward the carriage. He jumped into the seat next to her. "I wanted to tell you that I talked to my father tonight. There will be changes in my kingdom, I promise," he said seriously, referring to the conversation Keira had had with him and the duke about women holding office. He didn't realize he wasn't speaking to the same princess.

Tori looked at Liam, puzzled. She had no idea what he was talking about. She suddenly heard Riff bark. "Uh, that's nice," she said to Liam blankly. "Jump in, Riff!"

"Hyah!" Tori shouted as she cracked the whip. The carriage took off. They raced down the road, and Riff stuck his head out the side, happily letting his tongue hang out as the wind blew in his face.

Liam held on for dear life. "Are we rushing anywhere in particular?" he asked.

"I've got to rescue a magical diamond plant! And I think my best friend's in trouble!" Tori replied as the carriage careened around hairpin turns and over ancient cobblestone roads.

"Uh . . . okay, fine. Forget I asked," said Liam.

Tori and Liam arrived at the castle gate just as Rupert and Crider were making their escape past the guards, who had been knocked unconscious. Tori spotted the drooping gardenia plant. It was sticking out of Crider's bag.

"Excuse me, but I think that belongs to my kingdom!" said Tori as she and Liam jumped out of the carriage. Riff followed, growling at Crider and Rupert.

Crider turned to run, but another princess blocked his way.

"Going somewhere?" Keira asked. Vanessa growled at her side.

Crider was startled, and Rupert's jaw dropped. Tori looked like herself again—and Keira looked like her, too!

"There's two of them!" Crider yelled as he shoved Rupert aside.

Prince Liam looked back and forth between the two princesses, just as confused. "Um, which one of you do I like?" he asked.

"Her," Tori said, pointing to Keira.

Keira moved toward Crider, a smirk on her face. "Now, why don't you hand over that plant like a good little creep, Seymour?" she said.

Crider was stunned when he suddenly realized who he was talking to. "Keira?" he asked.

Rupert looked at Crider, dumbstruck by his boss's real name. "Seymour?"

"Don't call me that!" Crider screamed. Rupert took off running, and Riff eagerly lunged for him, sinking his teeth into one of Rupert's shoes. Rupert tripped and thudded to the ground. He scrambled to his feet in a panic and grabbed a sword from an unconscious guard.

Liam grabbed the other guard's sword and disarmed Rupert. Suddenly, Keira shouted, "Crider's getting away!"

Tori whipped around to see Crider jumping into the limo with the plant. He tried to start it, but the engine just chugged pitifully.

Vanessa stood near the car, chewing on the ignition wires, which she had just taken. Keira laughed as she leaned on the limo. "Aw, gee, that *is* tough, Seymour. No getaway car."

Crider looked around desperately. Then his face brightened. "Good thing the princess brought me a spare!" He leaped out of the limo, shoved Keira aside, and jumped into the royal carriage. Soon he was racing off with the plant.

Chapter 21

The girls ran after Crider's carriage while Liam stayed behind to guard Rupert. But they couldn't catch up.

"He got away!" Keira said, breathless.

"Not yet, he didn't!" Tori replied. She sprinted toward the edge of a nearby cliff, Keira following closely behind her. Strands of lights on a cable stretched from the cliff to the marina below. Tori could see Crider's carriage speeding down a winding road beneath the cable. The plant was in the seat next to him.

Tori whipped the chain belt off her concert costume and looped it over the cable.

"No!" screamed Keira when she saw what Tori was doing.

"It's the only way to catch up to him!" Tori

yelled as she wrapped her hands around the ends of the chain belt so she was hanging from the overhead cable. Then she pushed off from the cliff and slid down the cable, using it like a zip line.

"You're completely insane!" Keira yelled. She looked over the edge again. The enormous height almost made her dizzy. She backed away and was startled when her phone suddenly rang. "Hello?"

It was Limburger, and he was furious. "Where are you?" he bellowed. "What kind of intermission is this? Don't you know this broadcast is costing a hundred thousand dollars a minute? If you're not back here in five minutes, your live special is over! And you can kiss your career goodbye!"

Keira looked at her phone, then at Tori sliding down the zip line. She took a deep breath and tossed the phone off the cliff.

High over the gorge, Tori was zipping down the cable toward Crider's carriage as it sped down the side of the cliff. Just before Crider reached a sharp curve, Tori dropped from the sky and landed in a crouch in front of the carriage. The carriage horse reared up, whinnied, and slid to a halt.

"What in the world—?" asked Crider as Tori faced the carriage defiantly.

"I'll take that plant, and the diamonds, Mr. Crider," Tori said.

Crider shook his head. "Sorry, Princess. They're going with me. But you're not!" He cracked his whip, causing the horse to rear up over Tori.

"That's a no-no, Seymour!" Keira yelled suddenly. Crider looked up to see Keira whooshing down the zip line toward him. She dropped onto Crider feetfirst, knocking him out of the carriage.

Keira quickly grabbed the plant. "Got it!" she yelled to Tori.

Crider jumped to his feet and sprinted to the

edge of the roadside cliff. When he took off his coat, Keira and Tori were shocked to see that he was wearing a parachute suit underneath!

"Keep your crummy plant! I've still got the diamonds! Gotta fly!" Crider shouted as he waved the bag of diamonds at them, then leaped off the cliff. His parachute helped him to glide on the air currents toward the marina, where his boat was waiting.

The girls ran to the edge of the cliff. "I can't believe it. We lost him again!" Tori cried.

Crider swooped back toward the girls, taunting them as he flew a few feet over their heads. "You see, ladies, the trick is to always come prepared for anything! And it helps to have just the right outfit!" he called.

Keira had an idea. She pulled out her magic microphone. "The man's right," she said to Tori. "What always cheers me up is a new dress!" She pointed her microphone at Crider and shouted, "Ball Gown Number Fourteen!" A cloud of sparkles surrounded Crider in midair. When the cloud disappeared, Crider was wearing a poufy ball gown instead of his flying suit. He began to plummet.

"Noooooo!" Crider yelled. In his panic, he dropped the bag of diamonds and heard a splash as it hit the water below.

"Oh, no! The diamonds!" Tori said, gasping.

Crider's ball gown puffed out like a parachute, slowing his fall. He moaned as he slowly drifted down toward the amphitheater, where the audience was growing restless as they waited for Keira to return to the stage.

When the crowd saw a figure floating toward the stage, they cheered, thinking it was Keira. But as soon as they saw that it wasn't the pop star, they began to boo. The boos turned to laughter when Crider got caught in the rigging above the stage and was stuck dangling there in his gown.

♪

Inside the video-control trailer, Mr. Limburger was waiting for Keira to return to the stage. He looked at his watch as Nora stuck her head in the door. "No sign of her yet, Mr. Limburger," she reported.

Mr. Limburger scowled and picked up his intercom. "All right, boys," he said, "pack up the equipment. This broadcast is over. Keira's history."

Chapter 22

Tori and Keira rushed the wilted gardenia back to the secret garden and tried to replant it. As they patted down the dirt around it, the now-freed garden fairies hovered over it worriedly. Vanessa and Riff looked on, too, as the poor plant fell over. Tori shook her head sadly. "It's no use," she said with a sigh. "It's dead."

"Can't you plant another one?" Keira asked.

"No, its diamonds were its seeds," Tori replied. "If there were any diamonds left, we could plant them. But the last ones fell into the sea." Tori sat down on a nearby rock, and Vanessa put her head sadly in the princess's lap. "And it's all my fault."

"What was your fault, that Crider was born a jerk?" Keira asked as she sat next to Tori.

Behind them, the fairies gave the fallen plant a royal burial. They covered it with a mound of soil, then sadly sprinkled it with flower petals.

"No," Tori said. "It was my fault that I couldn't keep my kingdom safe. I didn't even know my subjects were in trouble. Some princess, huh?"

Keira sighed. "You're not so bad. I've been a princess for just two days and I nearly started a war—or at least a really bad argument."

Tori stood up and began to pace. "Yes, but princessing is my job, not yours," she said to Keira. "I haven't exactly been living up to it."

"Whoa," Keira said with a smile. "Don't grow up too fast. Who's going to teach me how to play the best pranks ever?"

Tori looked at Keira with concern. "I'm afraid you'll have lots of time to learn now, with no singing career."

Keira shrugged. "I was ready. It's time for me to get back to the music, even if it means singing in coffeehouses." She absentmindedly leaned over to pick a flower, but one of the fairies zipped in front of her face and shook a reproving finger at her. Keira nodded and backed off.

Tori smiled. "You'll always be a star, wherever you sing."

"Thanks," Keira replied. "At least I've started writing songs again—now that I've learned the secret."

"What secret?" Tori asked.

Keira grinned. "Pillow fights!"

Tori looked at her quizzically. "I'm so glad we got to be friends," she said.

"Yeah," Keira agreed. Suddenly, both girls' faces lit up. Their hands had gone to their necks. "The friendship necklaces!" they said at the same time. Vanessa perked up. The fairies excitedly swarmed back to the girls and helped them unclasp the necklaces and unstring the diamonds.

"Diamonds from the Diamond Gardenia!" Tori said excitedly.

Keira nodded. "Seeds!"

The girls quickly planted the two diamond seeds side by side. They waited for a moment, but nothing happened. Then the fairies buzzed in and watered the little mounds of dirt. Instantly, the seeds began to sprout, producing two tiny, glittering Diamond Gardenia plants!

"It worked!" Tori exclaimed.

"Double!" said Keira with a smile.

The lights inside the secret garden began to brighten again. Outside, the kingdom was coming back to life, too. The lights glowed more brightly, flowers opened, trees sprouted new leaves, and the garden waterfall cascaded down again.

Keira and Tori hugged as Vanessa and Riff woofed happily. Then the dogs leaned into each other and howled musically. The girls looked at each other, perplexed. "Are they . . . *singing*?" Keira asked.

"The concert!" they suddenly remembered.

Tori and Keira raced to the royal carriage. Tori took the reins and drove the carriage down the hill at breakneck speed. Next to her, Keira used the magical hairbrush and microphone to change both girls completely back to their true selves. "What if everyone left?" Keira asked.

"They'll be there," Tori replied confidently. "Record company or not, you've still got fans who love you. So don't disappoint them—finish the show."

Chapter 23

At the amphitheater, the audience waited faithfully for Keira to return to the stage. They were clapping their hands and chanting her name. “Keira! Keira! Keira!” Crider, still in his ball gown, scowled as he was led away by the palace guards.

A moment later, the crowd burst into a tremendous roar—Keira was back! She took her guitar from its stand and turned to the audience. The cheers were deafening.

“Hi!” Keira shouted. “Thanks for being so patient. I’d like to dedicate this next song to my two new sisters, Princesses Trevi and Meredith.”

In the royal box, the girls grinned widely. Then they jumped to their feet and shrieked with excitement.

After handing Rupert over to the palace guards, Liam returned to the box. He smiled and waved to Keira onstage. Keira smiled back at him and began to sing her closing song, "Look How High We Can Fly," accompanied only by her guitar. The audience listened, delighted. Keira kept strumming as she addressed the crowd. "I think this would sound great as a duet. Please welcome my best friend, Her Royal Highness Princess Tori!"

Tori walked onstage, surprised but grinning. Keira handed her another glimmering guitar. The royal family and Prince Liam looked on in shock. Then Liam and the young princesses started applauding. The king and the duchess joined in, followed by the cheering audience.

Keira and Tori smiled and launched into Keira's song as a duet:

"I found myself today,
And now I'm glad to say
I'm living life straight from the heart.
Oh, what a gift, you see.

I'm lucky to be me.
And now I just can't wait to start.
Look how high we can fly!
Look how high we can fly!
It's a beautiful view
From up here in the sky.
There's nothing we can't do
Together, me and you.
Look how high we can fly."

The audience responded with thunderous applause. During an instrumental break, Keira leaned over to Tori. "You know, singing in coffeehouses has some perks—like really great pastries. Feel like joining me? We make a pretty good team."

"We do," Tori told her, "but I've got some important stuff to take care of right here in my kingdom. And it's time I paid attention to it."

Keira understood. The girls turned back to their audience and continued with another duet. They created an unforgettable evening for their fans—and for each other.

"Here we are,
Being who we want,
Giving what we got.
Never a doubt now.

"Here we go,
Burning like a spark
Light up the dark
Again, again, again."

At the end of the night, the audience erupted in applause as Tori and Keira left the stage together, glad to be themselves once again.